# YO-KAI WATCH™

## It's YO-KAI WATCH Time:
# PUZZLES AND FRIENDS

**LITTLE, BROWN & COMPANY**
## LB kids

New York  Boston

This book is a work of fiction. Names, characters, places, and incidents are the product of the author's imagination or are used fictitiously. Any resemblance to actual events, locales, or persons, living or dead, is coincidental.

©LEVEL-5/YWP. ©2016 LEVEL-5 Inc.

In accordance with the U.S. Copyright Act of 1976, the scanning, uploading, and electronic sharing of any part of this book without the permission of the publisher is unlawful piracy and theft of the author's intellectual property. If you would like to use material from the book (other than for review purposes), prior written permission must be obtained by contacting the publisher at permissions@hbgusa.com. Thank you for your support of the author's rights.

Little, Brown and Company
Hachette Book Group
1290 Avenue of the Americas, New York, NY 10104
Visit us at lb-kids.com

Little, Brown and Company is a division of Hachette Book Group, Inc. The Little, Brown name and logo are trademarks of Hachette Book Group, Inc.

The publisher is not responsible for websites (or their content) that are not owned by the publisher.

First Edition: October 2016

ISBN 978-0-316-36107-1

10 9 8 7 6 5 4 3 2 1

LSC-C

Printed in the United States of America

# This book belongs to:

---

# How it all began...

One day a boy named Nate Adams discovered something in the mountains—Mount Wildwood to be precise—that would change his life forever! After putting a coin into a strange vending machine, a capsule came out. Inside the capsule was…

a Yo-kai named Whisper!
Whisper gave Nate a
special Yo-kai Watch. The
watch allows Nate to see
the Yo-kai that are hidden
all around the world.
Whenever Nate meets
and becomes friends
with a Yo-kai, they give him
a medal for his watch as a
symbol of their friendship.
Nate can call upon his
Yo-kai friends whenever he needs their help.
In this special activity book, you will
learn all about the Yo-kai! You will
be quizzed on your super
knowledge, and asked to
complete some zany puzzles.

## Are you up for the challenge?

Before we jump in and learn all about the Yo-kai, here are some things to know about Nate. We're not just going to give it to you, though! It won't be that easy, my friend! Can you unscramble the letters to find out about average Nate?

**This is the grade Nate is in:**

T I H F F

_ _ _ _ _

**Bet you didn't know Nate is a nickname! His full first name is:**

H T A N N A

_ _ _ _ _ _

**This is where Nate discovered the vending machine that brought Whisper to him:**

T O M U N   D W D O D O L I W

_ _ _ _ _   _ _ _ _ _ _ _ _

**This is what Nate uses to see Yo-kai: His**

O Y – I K A   C W T H A

_ _ – _ _ _   _ _ _ _ _

## What words can you create using the
## letters from Nate's name?

# NATE ADAMS

Yo-kai have different skills and strengths based on the Tribe they are in. That's how they stir up trouble…or how they get through their day-to-day Yo-kai life.

**What is something you are really good at?**
**Draw a picture of you showing your skill below:**

As you probably know, Yo-kai are divided into eight Tribes, listed below. But the vowels are missing from the Tribe names. Is this the work of a Yo-kai?

**Fill in the missing vowels in the Tribe names and put an end to this nonsense!**

SL_PP_RY

MYST_R___S

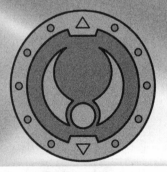

BR_V_

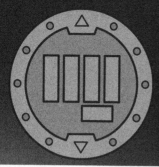

**T__GH**

**H__RTF_L**

**CH__RM__NG**

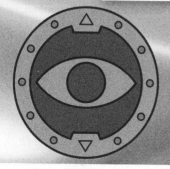

**__R__**

**SH_DY**

Whisper considers himself to be the "Yo-kai butler" and an expert on all things Yo-kai. Though, with the way he always struggles to find info about anything, it really makes you wonder. Let's see if you know more than Whisper!

## Which two images of Whisper are exactly the same? Circle them!

You and Whisper are now friends, and he has given you the Yo-kai Watch!

# CONGRATULATIONS!

Now that you have the Yo-kai Watch from Whisper, you can see all Yo-kai. Color the pictures and get to know them in these wacky quizzes! You can turn back to these pages whenever you pull a Whisper and need help answering quiz questions!

# CHARMING

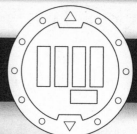

# HEARTFUL

# SHADY

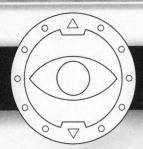

# EERIE

# BRAVE

# SLIPPERY

This Yo-kai is Nate's best friend and someone he calls on all the time. They met when this Yo-kai was training to become strong enough to defeat trucks. He often yells "Paws of Fury" when he battles.

**Can you figure out who the Yo-kai is from the silhouette?**

You got it! Did you take a peek for answers anywhere? No? Well then, how about this:

**Unscramble the letters to find out which Tribe he belongs to:**

# G N C H A M R I

— — — — — — — — —

Let's find out a little more about him!

**Can you spot the differences between when he was a regular cat and a Yo-kai?**

Now that you know Jibanyan a little more, he needs your help! Jibanyan's favorite group, Next HarMEOWny, is performing soon, but he can't decide on the items he needs for the concert.

**Circle the correct items so he can make it in time!**

**PILLOW**

**POSTER**

**APPLE**

**AUTOGRAPH BOOK**

**CONCERT TICKET**

What a fun day at the concert! Jibanyan has fallen asleep. Looks like our charming Yo-kai is dreaming of his favorite snack—chocobars!

**Draw a picture of what Jibanyan is dreaming of:**

As you probably know by now, Jibanyan likes meeting new friends! He's a bit of a lazy fella, but that's how cats are.

**Draw a picture of yourself having an adventure or just a relaxing afternoon with Jibanyan.**

Make sure you include his favorite snack, chocobars!

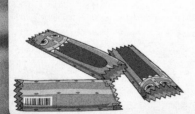

You and Jibanyan are now friends. As a symbol of friendship, you have received his medal!

# CONGRATULATIONS!

**Make sure you keep that safe.**
**You might need it later.**

These two Yo-kai are brothers, Komasan and Komajiro. The brothers aren't from the city, but they are part of the same Tribe that Jibanyan is in. Do you remember which Tribe that is?

**Pull up yer pants, put on your cowboy hat, and write it on the line below:**

-------------------------------------------------------------------

Whisper's Yo-kai Pad is malfunctioning!
What is he going to do now? It's time to test your
knowledge. Can you help him pick the correct
information about Komasan
and Komajiro? The brothers
are giving hints!

**Name:** Komasan

**Favorite food:**

Pizza

or

Ice Cream

**Name:** Komajiro

**Personality:**

Curious

or

Scared

Komasan and Komajiro both have lovely names that their mama gave them, which begin with the letter K.

**What other words can you think of that begins with the letter K? Write them on the lines below:**

---

---

---

---

---

---

---

---

---

You might have guessed, but Komasan is a country Yo-kai gettin' used to the ways of them city folk. What would you share with Komasan about where you live?

**Show Komasan how awesome your hometown is by drawing a picture of it!**

People confuse Komasan and Komajiro all the time, but can you recognize their differences?

**Circle the pictures that are Komasan and draw a triangle around the ones that are Komajiro.**

Komasan is showing his little brother around the city, but these two country folk get a little lost! Help them find their way to the restaurant to get some downright delicious ice cream!

**START**

**FINISH**

Komasan may not know much about the city, but Komajiro has a lot of respect for his big brother. Who is someone you look up to?

**Draw a picture of them and write their name below:**

You are now friends with Komasan and Komajiro! As a symbol of friendship, you have received their medals!

# CONGRATULATIONS!

This Yo-kai is Blazion! Ever feel the sudden need to do *everything*? That's probably Blazion inspiriting you. He emblazes people's hearts with motivation!

## Add flames to Blazion's mane of fire.

Blazion is a very brave Yo-kai. This is Blazion's Tribe medal.

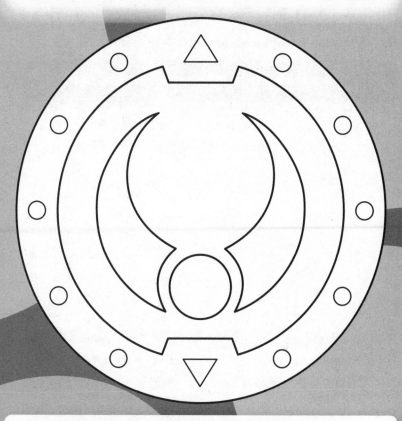

**Circle the name of the Tribe he belongs to.**
**This should be an easy one!**

SLIPPERY          EERIE          TOUGH

BRAVE          CHARMING          SHADY

MYSTERIOUS          HEARTFUL

Let's talk more about Blazion's inspiriting power. Blazion is motivating these people to do well at their activities. What is the effect that he will have on these lazy daisies?

## Draw a picture of what might happen.

*Nate has left his summer homework for the last day before school starts again.*

*Jibanyan throws his used chocobar wrapper on the floor.*

*Whisper doesn't feel like looking up information on a new Yo-kai.*

Nate was having a hard time getting motivated to do his homework, so he called on Blazion to help him out. Now Nate is ready to go, but his notes are scrambled!

**Help unscramble the letters to see which subjects Nate has to study:**

## T H M A

\_\_ \_\_ \_\_ \_\_

## G R P Y H O E G A

\_\_ \_\_ \_\_ \_\_ \_\_ \_\_ \_\_ \_\_ \_\_

## G I L E H N S

\_\_ \_\_ \_\_ \_\_ \_\_ \_\_ \_\_

## I E S N C C E

\_\_ \_\_ \_\_ \_\_ \_\_ \_\_ \_\_

Nice job! You and Blazion are now friends! As a symbol of friendship, you have received his medal!

# CONGRATULATIONS!

Does this Yo-kai look a little familiar? He is a robotic version of one of the other Yo-kai…but from the future!

## Circle the Yo-kai you think he looks similar to:

Robonyan has a strong, upgraded body that allows him to battle even the toughest of trucks.

## Pick a move for Robonyan to use on these trucks.

## Draw the outcome of the battle!

All right, let's see if you're paying attention! The Tribe Robonyan is in rhymes with "rough." Do you know what his Tribe is?

**Write it on the line below:**

---

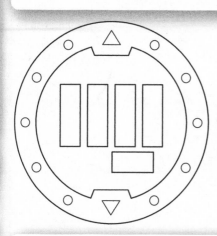

Yup! You got it again. Boy, at this rate you're going to know more than Whisper! Let's test you! Do you know any other Yo-kai in the Tough Tribe?

**Write their names on the line below:**

---

---

Sweet! Now, imagine you come from the future like Robonyan.

**Draw a picture of what you would look like.**

Wow! You are going to look awesome. Because Robonyan is a robot, he doesn't have emotions. But you are not a robot (at least not yet!), so you have emotions.

**Circle the words below that are emotions:**

HAPPY

TIRED

HUNGRY

SAD

TALL

MAD

YOUNG

OLD

FURRY

STINKY

SPONGY

AFRAID

Uh-oh! Jibanyan is all out of chocobars.
Guide the chocobars through the factory within
Robonyan so Jibanyan can have his favorite treat!

You did it! You and Robonyan are now friends! As a symbol of friendship, you have received his medal!

# CONGRATULATIONS!

**Draw a picture of Robonyan's medal to add it to your collection.**

It's time to color-in-a-kai! You can stay true to the original, or change things up by coloring the Yo-kai differently. The choice is yours.

All right, time for a quick quiz to see if you're paying attention! Match the Yo-kai to their Tribe!

**HERE'S A TIP:** Two of the Tribes
don't have any matches yet. Don't be fooled!

You did it! Okay, one more thing before we meet more friends. Can you find the names of the Yo-kai you have met so far—and their Tribes—in the word search? Words can be forward, backward, and even up and down!

## Circle the words below:

```
W  V  G  Q  O  B  Z  I  F  V  A  Z
H  Q  N  K  R  Y  H  Y  O  C  O  B
U  R  I  N  I  N  G  T  Q  V  A  A
U  O  M  V  J  A  U  K  N  C  Y  Y
B  B  R  T  A  Y  O  M  A  R  O  N
D  O  A  Z  M  N  T  H  S  K  N  O
K  N  H  Y  O  A  L  U  A  Y  G  I
C  Y  C  G  K  B  Y  V  M  X  B  Z
D  A  Y  B  X  I  V  T  O  O  T  A
K  N  K  N  T  J  J  I  K  I  Q  L
E  R  E  P  S  I  H  W  C  G  E  B
O  O  E  B  R  A  V  E  V  X  K  A
```

| Whisper | Blazion | Brave |
| Jibanyan | Komasan | Charming |
| Robonyan | Komajiro | Tough |

Now you are ready to
meet more Yo-kai!

This Yo-kai is a warrior and Jibanyan's ancestor. Fill in the missing vowels below to spell his name:

**SH_G_NY_N**

**Fill in the missing vowels to see this Yo-kai's Tribe and how rare he is:**

**BR_V_**

**L_G_ND_RY**

Shogunyan battles with his trusty sword, but it is missing!

**Draw Shogunyan's sword and see if you can help him split these foods perfectly between Nate, Whisper, and himself.**

Hey! I'm not food!

You and Shogunyan are now friends! As a symbol of friendship, you have received his medal! Congratulations!

# CONGRATULATIONS!

**Draw a picture of Shogunyan's medal to add it to your collection.**

There is a version of Jibanyan you have yet to meet! But first, Whisper wants to test your knowledge!

## Match the names of the Yo-kai with their pictures:

ROBONYAN

SHOGUNYAN

JIBANYAN

This version of Jibanyan is bad to the bone! Jibanyan becomes this way when he gets inspirited by another Yo-kai named Roughraff. Make sure you watch your chocobars, because this cat doesn't follow the rules!

## HIS NAME IS BADDINYAN.

**Baddinyan is in the same Tribe as Jibanyan.**
**Can you remember what Tribe that is?**
**Write it on the line below:**

⋯⋯⋯⋯⋯⋯⋯⋯⋯⋯⋯⋯⋯⋯⋯⋯⋯⋯⋯⋯⋯⋯

The bad in Baddinyan isn't all big talk!
At least, he likes to think so. Even baddies
like Baddinyan have a code of honor!

## What are the rules you live by? List them out below.

Baddinyan and Jibanyan are pretty much the same, but they look different! In the pictures below, circle all of the things that are different about them.

Your knowledge has earned Baddinyan's respect. You and Baddinyan are now friends! As a symbol of friendship, you have received his medal!

# CONGRATULATIONS!

**Draw a picture of Baddinyan's medal to add it to your collection.**

This Yo-kai is Venoct. Venoct fights with his dragon scarf.

## Connect the dots to see Venoct's amazing scarf!

Do you know what Tribe Venoct belongs to?

# YPPISELR

\_\_ \_\_ \_\_ \_\_ \_\_ \_\_ \_\_ \_\_

**Venoct seems to be in a bit of a bind! Draw his dragon scarf to fend off his enemies!**

If you were faced with a super-strong foe, which Yo-kai friend would you call to your aid?

## Illustrate your epic battle in the comic strip below:

You and Venoct are now friends! As a symbol of friendship, you have received his medal!

# CONGRATULATIONS!

Draw a picture of Venoct's medal to add it to your collection.

This Yo-kai is Kyubi, and he is quite the charmer. He belongs to the Mysterious Tribe. Though he can transform into a human, his Yo-kai form has nine tails!

**Draw Kyubi's tails below:**

Kyubi has the power to control fire. His power is as strong as a volcanic eruption! However, is Kyubi more powerful than a volcano?

**Draw a picture of an erupting volcano below and see which produces more power—the volcano or Kyubi!**

You and Kyubi are now friends! As a symbol of friendship, you have received his medal.

# CONGRATULATIONS!

**Draw a picture of Kyubi's medal
to add it to your collection.**

This Yo-kai is Walkappa. He is in the Charming Tribe. Most kappas stay in the water, but Walkappa lives on land. He uses a water bottle to help him stay cool and happy.

Walkappa wants to play a game of connect-a-kai.

## Connect the dots to complete this picture of Walkappa!

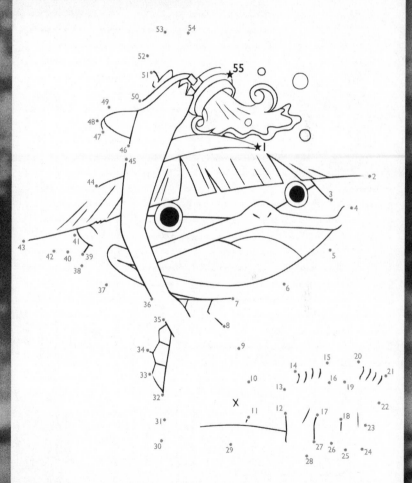

Oh, no! Walkappa lost his water bottle. He can't leave the water too long without it.

**Help him find it so he can explore a little more!**

START

FINISH

As you have learned, most kappas live in water. Let's take a breather and circle the animals below that also live in water.

CAT

SHARK

DOG

SHRIMP

LION

FROG

GOLDFISH

TIGER

COYOTE

FOX

WHALE

ZEBRA

Awesome! You and Walkappa are now friends! As a symbol of friendship, you have received his medal!

# CONGRATULATIONS!

**Draw a picture of Walkappa's medal
to add it to your collection.**

Walkappa is not the only
Yo-kai you are friends with
from the Charming Tribe!

**Draw a picture of another
Yo-kai from this Tribe:**

Are you ready to meet even more Yo-kai?

First let's see if you can list the names of all the Yo-kai you've met so far.

**Write their names below their pictures. If you need help, you can turn back and check the earlier pages of this book!**

- - - - - - - - - -     - - - - - - - - - -     - - - - - - - - - -     - - - - - - - - - -

- - - - - - - - - -          - - - - - - - - - -          - - - - - - - - - -

- - - - - - - - - -          - - - - - - - - - -          - - - - - - - - - -

You are friends with so many Yo-kai!

**Color the pictures below. Then use one word to describe each of your Yo-kai friends.**

-----------------  -----------------  -----------------  -----------------

-----------------  -----------------  -----------------

-----------------  -----------------  -----------------

This Yo-kai is Noway. He never wants to say yes to anything—he is always saying, "No way!" If he inspirits you, you will say, "No way!" to everything!

## Connect the dots to see this Tough Yo-kai.

Noway has inspirited you. What are some things you would say, "No way!" to? Write a big "No way!" on them.

These three Yo-kai love to dance! Use the code to figure
out what their names are and write them on the lines below:

| A 1 | J 10 | S 19 |
|-----|------|------|
| B 2 | K 11 | T 20 |
| C 3 | L 12 | U 21 |
| D 4 | M 13 | V 22 |
| E 5 | N 14 | W 23 |
| F 6 | O 15 | X 24 |
| G 7 | P 16 | Y 25 |
| H 8 | Q 17 | Z 26 |
| I 9 | R 18 | |

23 9 7 12 9 14

__ __ __ __ __ __

19 20 5 16 16 1

__ __ __ __ __ __

18 8 25 20 8

__ __ __ __ __

This Yo-kai is Noko. He is said to bring good luck. Look at his head. It's a four-leaf clover!

Sometimes good things and bad things can happen at the same time! Below are five examples of when the bad and good meet.

Buhu

**Fill in the lines to show how good things can come out of bad luck:**

Noko

| BAD LUCK: | GOOD LUCK: |
|---|---|
| I stepped in dog poop! | But I found $5 when I leaned down to clean my shoe! |
| I had a kale salad for dinner. Yuck! | |
| I missed the school bus! | |
| We had a surprise quiz in class today! | |
| I'm not allowed to eat chocolate before going to bed! | |

Read the sentences below and decide whether Nate is inspirited by Noko or Buhu (the Yo-kai that gives you bad luck!). Color the ovals orange for Noko and green for Buhu.

Nate finds a dollar on the street!

Nate loses his homework!

There is a big storm on the night of Nate's big sleepover, and the party is cancelled.

Nate's mom makes his favorite meal for dinner!

This Yo-kai is Insomni. If she inspirits you, you won't be able to fall asleep! I sure could go for a nap right now.

Insomni paid Nate a visit and now he can't fall asleep. Some say that counting sheep will help you to fall asleep. Have you ever tried that?

**Draw sheep for Nate to count:**

Imagine you have the power to stay awake all night! What would you do every night while everyone else was asleep?

**Draw a picture of it:**

Nate is still wide-awake! He could really use a good night's rest. You haven't met this Yo-kai yet, so unscramble the letters to find out which Yo-kai can help him have sweet dreams!

# U B K A

___ ___ ___ ___

You and Insomni are now friends! As a symbol of friendship, you have received her medal.

# CONGRATULATIONS!

**Draw a picture of Insomni's medal**
**to add it to your collection.**

This cheerful Yo-kai is Happierre. He has the power to cheer up even the angriest person! Happierre usually has a flower on top of his head, but it is missing right now!

**Draw in Happierre's flower to complete him!**

Happierre loves to make people feel happy.

## Draw a picture of the happiest person you know:

This Yo-kai is Dismarelda. She has the power to make even the happiest person put on a frown! But her husband, Happierre, helps cancel out her gloom and makes things normal again.

**Let's help Dismarelda get back her color! Color in Dismarelda:**

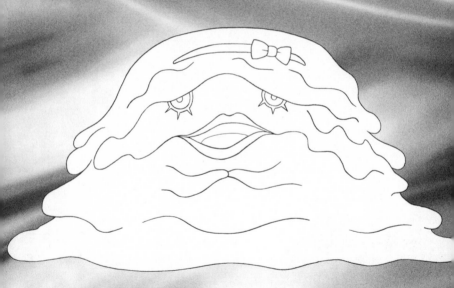

Happierre needs to get home to Dismarelda! Help him get through the maze so he can make it home in time for dinner!

START

FINISH

Now that you know what this Yo-kai couple is capable of, read the sentences below and decide if this is the work of Happierre or Dismarelda!

**A**
Nate is arguing with his best friend!

**B**
Nate did poorly on an exam, but he still feels good.

**C**
Nate is upset with Whisper!

**D**
Nate is happy to read a boring textbook!

**E**
Nate is not laughing at a funny joke.

You are now friends with Happierre and Dismarelda! As a symbol of friendship, you have received their medals.

# CONGRATULATIONS!

**Draw a picture of their medals to add them to your collection.**

This Yo-kai is Negatibuzz. Negatibuzz brings negativity!
He never sees the bright side of any situation.

**Negatibuzz's buzzing reminds Nate of a pesky insect. Unscramble the letters to see which insect he reminds Nate of:**

# O Q M S O T U I

\_\_\_ \_\_\_ \_\_\_ \_\_\_ \_\_\_ \_\_\_ \_\_\_ \_\_\_

Whisper wants to test your knowledge again! Can you find the names of the Yo-kai you have just met in the word search? Words can be forward, backward, and even up and down!

**Circle the words below:**

| | | | | | | | | | | |
|---|---|---|---|---|---|---|---|---|---|---|
| E | H | A | P | P | I | E | R | R | E | M | Z |
| T | K | R | M | T | N | O | W | A | Y | V | G |
| B | X | W | H | S | R | M | Y | U | H | F | M |
| S | A | C | J | Y | G | U | C | O | Z | P | G |
| Z | Z | U | B | I | T | A | G | E | N | J | B |
| N | O | K | O | N | F | H | U | Y | F | Q | J |
| X | W | C | R | M | R | M | S | S | Q | Q | F |
| S | F | I | O | O | K | P | D | W | M | F | X |
| G | X | P | G | S | T | E | P | P | A | F | D |
| Y | Q | O | R | N | Q | V | C | O | O | I | J |
| W | I | G | L | I | N | Z | W | M | K | X | Y |
| C | E | T | F | C | Q | X | A | M | B | J | W |

**Negatibuzz**   **Noko**   **Steppa**

**Happierre**   **Noway**   **Rhyth**

**Insomni**   **Wiglin**

This big, strong Yo-kai is named B3-NKI. He is half-machine!

**Do you know the word for something that is half-machine? Unscramble the letters below to find out:**

# G Y C O R B

\_\_ \_\_ \_\_ \_\_ \_\_ \_\_

Use the code to figure out the name of these Yo-kai you have not met yet:

| A 1 | H 8 | O 15 | V 22 |
| B 2 | I 9 | P 16 | W 23 |
| C 3 | J 10 | Q 17 | X 24 |
| D 4 | K 11 | R 18 | Y 25 |
| E 5 | L 12 | S 19 | Z 26 |
| F 6 | M 13 | T 20 | |
| G 7 | N 14 | U 21 | |

6   9   4   7   5   16   8   1   14   20

_   _   _   _   _   _   _   _   _   _

23   1   26   26   1   20

_   _   _   _   _   _

18   15   21   7   8   18   1   6   6

_   _   _   _   _   _   _   _   _

4   1   26   26   1   2   5   12

_   _   _   _   _   _   _   _

You're not finished yet! Use the code to figure out the
names of these Yo-kai as well!

| | | | | | | |
|---|---|---|---|---|---|---|
| **A** 1 | **H** 8 | **O** 15 | **V** 22 |
| **B** 2 | **I** 9 | **P** 16 | **W** 23 |
| **C** 3 | **J** 10 | **Q** 17 | **X** 24 |
| **D** 4 | **K** 11 | **R** 18 | **Y** 25 |
| **E** 5 | **L** 12 | **S** 19 | **Z** 26 |
| **F** 6 | **M** 13 | **T** 20 | |
| **G** 7 | **N** 14 | **U** 21 | |

4    9    13    13    25

__   __   __   __   __


8    9    4    1    2    1    20

__   __   __   __   __   __   __


20    1    20    20    12    5    20    5    12    12

__   __   __   __   __   __   __   __   __   __


8    21    14    7    18    1    13    16    19

__   __   __   __   __   __   __   __   __

Whisper wants to quiz you again! Prove to him that you don't need to look at the Yo-kai Pad like he always does. (But don't worry! You can turn back to the previous pages in this book if you need help.)

**Unscramble the letters to find out the name of the Tribe Whisper wants to quiz you about first:**

# E R A H F L U T

—— —— —— —— —— —— —— ——

**Write one fact you know about a Yo-kai from this Tribe:**

---------------------------------------

---------------------------------------

---------------------------------------

---------------------------------------

---------------------------------------

---------------------------------------

Write the name of
the Tribe these Yo-kai
belong to:

---------------------------

**Write one fact you know about
a Yo-kai from this Tribe:**

Study the Tribe icons on this page. Then turn this page and see if you can match the Tribe names to the icons!

**BRAVE**     **MYSTERIOUS**     **TOUGH**

**HEARTFUL**     **SHADY**     **EERIE**

**CHARMING**     **SLIPPERY**

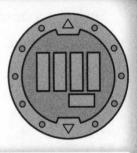

Whisper's Yo-kai Pad is malfunctioning again! Help Whisper figure out who this Yo-kai is by drawing in the grayed-out areas!

Dimmy

Being inspirited by this Yo-kai will dim your presence.

You won't be noticed, just like a ninja!

Wiglin, Steppa, and Rhyth can't stop dancing! Fill in the missing vowels in the words below to see the names of some different types of dancing:

B _ _ LL _ T

T _ _ P

SQ _ _ _ _ R _ _
D _ NC _ _ NG

Tattletell is a Yo-kai who will inspirit you to tell her *all* of your secrets! What secrets is Tattletell revealing about Nate's classmates?

### Katie:

### Bear:

### Eddie:

I actually don't know anything about Yo-kai unless I check the Yo-kai Pad!

I love chocobars and Next HarMEOWny!

What words can you make using the letters from the names of these Yo-kai?

**TATTLETELL    STEPPA    RHYTH    WIGLIN**

Hungramps is a Yo-kai who will make your tummy rumble! Nate is hungry after seeing Hungramps! Draw some food on the plate for Nate to eat, but don't let Hungramps get too close or else Nate will eat more than he can handle!

Can you identify the Yo-kai from the pictures below?

A

B

C

D

Study the picture at the top of the page of the Shady Yo-kai.
Then look at the picture on the bottom of the page. It looks
similar, but some items are missing.

## What items are missing?

Which Yo-kai will you call?

**Read the situations below and help Nate decide which Yo-kai to call for help:**

**Nate needs help feeling brave enough to talk to Katie.**

--------------------------------

--------------------------------

**Nate needs help staying awake to finish his homework.**

--------------------------------

--------------------------------

**Nate needs help confronting a powerful Yo-kai.**

--------------------------------

--------------------------------

Can you identify the Yo-kai from their silhouette?

Look carefully! Which picture of Jibanyan is different than the others? Circle it!

Here are seven Whispers each ready to take on a different color of the rainbow!

**Bonus points if you choose the colors
in the same order as a rainbow.**

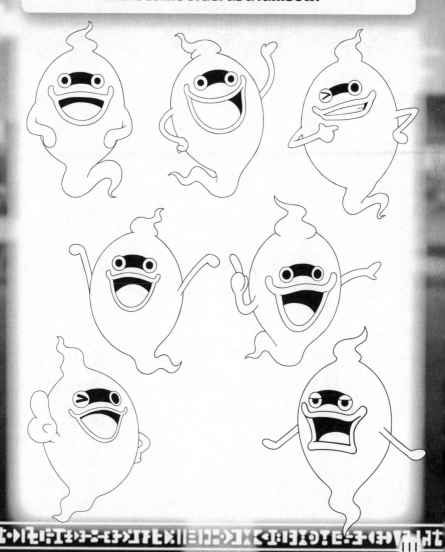

Whisper wants to quiz you one last time to see if you're worthy of the title EXECUTIVE YO-KAI EXPERT! Are you ready?

**Write your answers on the lines below Whisper's questions. Remember, if you need help, it's okay to turn back to the earlier pages in your book!**

**1.** Which Yo-kai is from the future?

_____

**2.** Which Yo-kai has a mane of fire?

_____

**3.** Which Yo-kai has nine tails?

_____

**4.** Which two Yo-kai are brothers?

_____

_____

**5.** Which Yo-kai prevents you from falling asleep?

**6.** Which Yo-kai uses a water bottle to keep himself wet?

**7.** Which Yo-kai has a dragon scarf?

**8.** Which Yo-kai is bad to the bone?

**9.** Which Yo-kai brings good luck?

**10.** Which Yo-kai will make you hungry?

**EXTRA CREDIT BONUS QUESTION!** *(Try to answer this one without looking back for help if you can!)*

Circle all the Yo-kai who don't belong in the Charming Tribe.

**BUHU**

**JIBANYAN**

**ROBONYAN**

**WHISPER**

**VENOCT**

**WALKAPPA**

**INSOMNI**

**KOMAJIRO**

**BADDINYAN**

**BLAZION**

**WAZZAT**

**KOMASAN**

You have collected so many Yo-kai medals that you can keep them organized in this encyclopedia!

**Which medal is the most special one in your entire collection?**

----------------------------------------

# ANSWER KEY

**Page 5**

Fifth

Nathan

Mount Wildwood

Yo-kai Watch

**Page 8**

SL<u>I</u>PP<u>E</u>RY

MYSTE<u>R</u><u>IOU</u>S

BR<u>A</u>VE

**Page 9**

T<u>OU</u>GH

HE<u>A</u>RT<u>FU</u>L

CHA<u>R</u>M<u>I</u>NG

<u>EE</u>R<u>I</u>E

SH<u>A</u>DY

**Page 10**

**B** and **F** are the same.

**Page 20**

The sillouette is Jibanyan.

He belongs to the CHARMING tribe.

**Page 21**

Yo-kai Jibanyan has two fiery tails, a yellow belly warmer, can walk on his hind legs, and has a piece missing from his left ear.

**Page 22**

Poster, Concert Ticket, Autograph Book

## Page 26
Charming

## Page 27
Ice Cream
Curious

## Page 30
A, C, E and G are Komasan.
B, D, F and H are Komajiro.

## Page 31

## Page 35
BRAVE

**Page 37**

MATH

GEOGRAPHY

ENGLISH

SCIENCE

**Page 39**

**Page 41**

TOUGH

Noway, Fidgephant, and Roughraff.

**Page 43**

Happy, Sad, Mad, and Afraid.

**Page 44**

**Page 50**

**Page 51**

```
W V G Q O B Z I F V A Z
H Q N K R Y H Y O C O B
U R I N I N G T Q V A A
U O M V J A U K N C Y Y
B B R T A Y O M A R O N
D O A Z M N T H S K N O
K N H Y O A L U A Y G I
C Y C G K B Y V M X B Z
D A Y B X I V T O O T A
K N K N T J J I K I Q L
E R E P S I H W C G E B
O O E B R A V E V X K A
```

**Page 53**

SH<u>O</u>GUNY<u>A</u>N

BR<u>A</u>V<u>E</u>

LE<u>G</u>END<u>A</u>RY

**Page 56**

ROBONYAN

SHOGUNYAN

JIBANYAN

**Page 57**

CHARMING

## Page 59

## Page 61

## Page 62

SLIPPERY

## Page 69

**Page 70**

**Page 71**

Shark, Shrimp, Frog, Goldfish, and Whale.

**Page 75**

*Top line* – Walkappa, Jibanyan, Robonyan, Baddinyan.

*Middle line* – Whisper, Venoct, Blazion.

*Bottom line* – Komasan, Komajiro, Kyubi.

**Page 76**

**Page 77**

WIGLIN

STEPPA

RHYTH

## Page 80

Nate finds a dollar on the street!—NOKO

Nate loses his homework!—BUHU

There is a big storm on the night of Nate's big sleepover, and the party is canceled.—BUHU

Nate's mom makes his favorite meal for dinner!—NOKO

## Page 84

BAKU

## Page 89

## Page 90

Happierre – B and D

Dismarelda – A, C, and E

## Page 107

## Page 108

Blazion

Insomni

B3-NKI or Kyubi or Venoct

## Page 109

**A** Fidgephant

**B** Walkappa

**C** B3-NKI

**D** Happierre

## Page 110

D is different. Jibanyan has no collar.

## Page 112

1. Robonyan

2. Blazion

3. Kyubi

4. Komasan and Komajiro

## Page 113

5. Insomni

6. Walkappa

7. Venoct

8. Baddinyan

9. Noko

10. Hungramps

## Page 114:

**These Yo-kai are not in the Charming Tribe!**

Buhu

Robonyan

Whisper

Venoct

Walkappa

Insomni

Blazion

Wazzat